Help me, Herman.

Herman the Helper

BY ROBERT KRAUS

PICTURES BY
JOSE ARUEGO & ARIANE DEWEY

SCHOLASTIC INC.

New York Toronto London Auckland Sydney
Mexico City New Delhi Hong Kong

Don't worry, I'll help you.

Text copyright © 1974 by Robert Kraus.
Illustrations copyright © 1974 by Jose Aruego and Ariane Dewey.
All rights reserved. Published by Scholastic Inc., 555 Broadway, New York, NY 10012,
by arrangement with Robert Kraus, Jose Aruego and Ariane Dewey.
SCHOLASTIC and associated logos and designs are
trademarks and/or registered trademarks of Scholastic Inc.

Printed in the U.S.A.

ISBN 0-439-08630-2

10 09 08 07 06 05   14   10 09 08 07 06 05

For Pamela, Bruce, Billy & Juan

4

Herman liked to help.

Thank you, Herman.

He helped his mother.

That's nice, Herman.

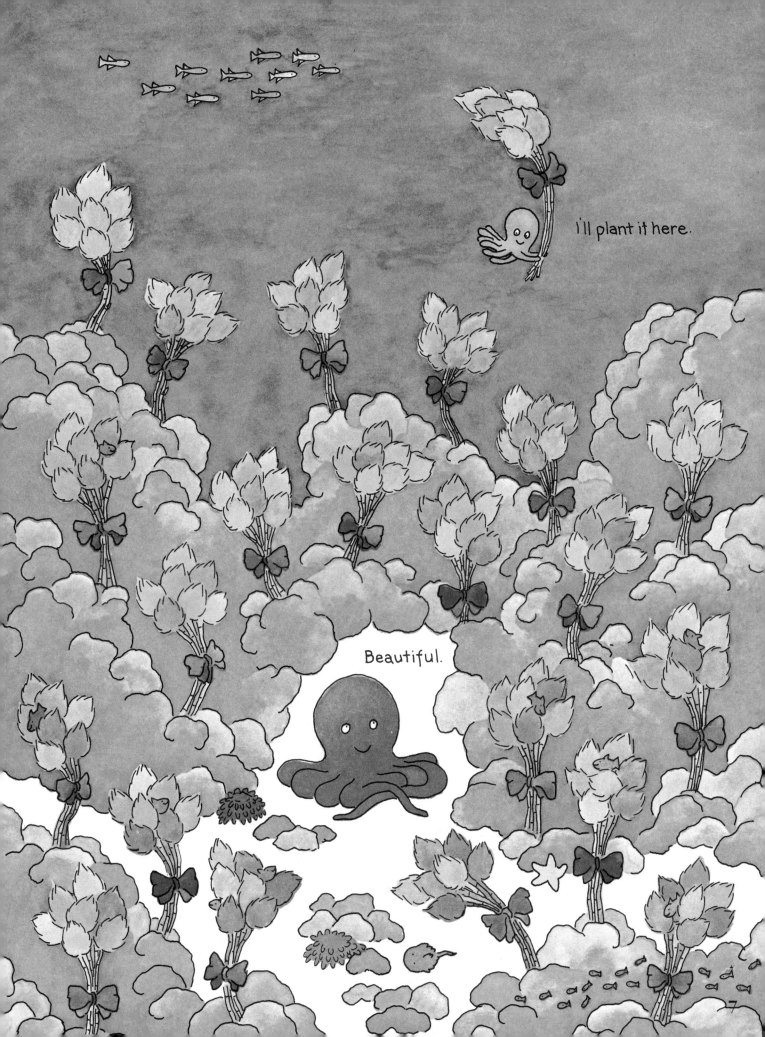

He helped his father.

Hide me, Herman.

Good hunting, Dad.

8

That's my dad.

He helped his brothers and sisters.

Thank you, brother.

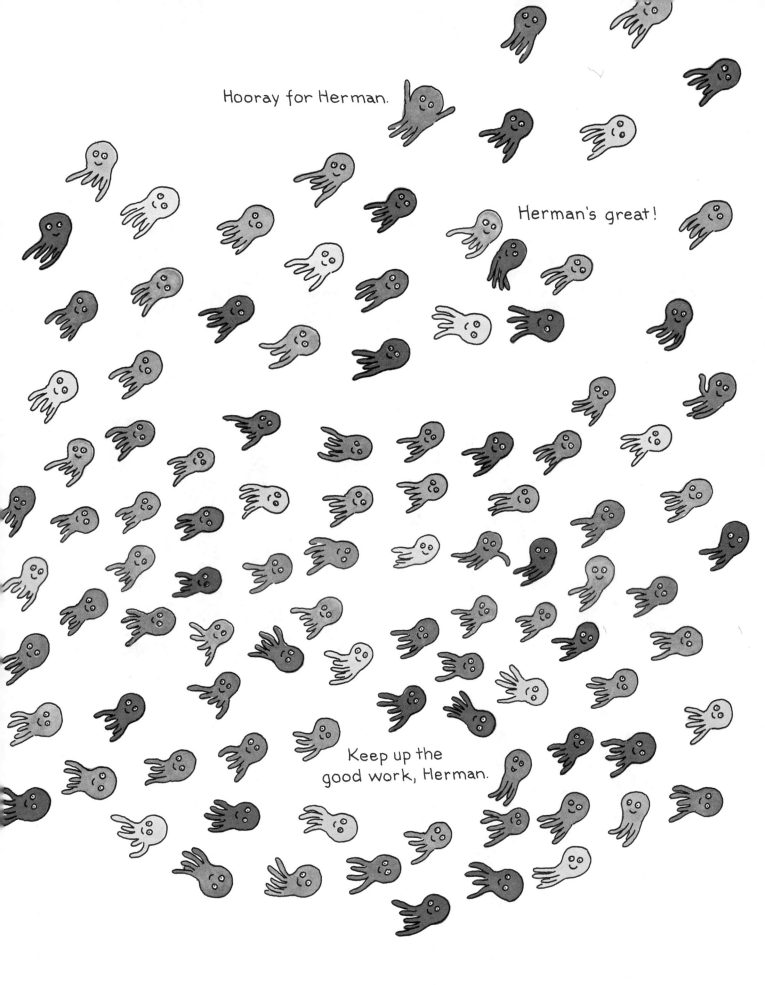

He helped his aunt.

What a beautiful bonnet, Herman.

Yes.

He helped his uncle.

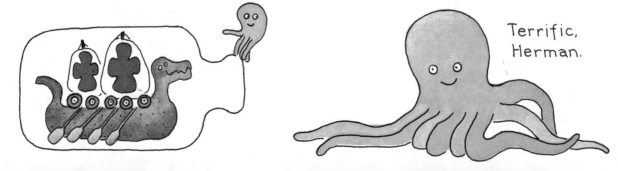

How's that, Uncle?

Terrific, Herman.

He helped his friends.

Take it easy, Herman.

Many thanks, Herman.

He helped his enemies.

Okay.

Help! It's after us!

I'll camouflage you with my ink.

sissssssssss

Herman saved the day!

He helped the young.

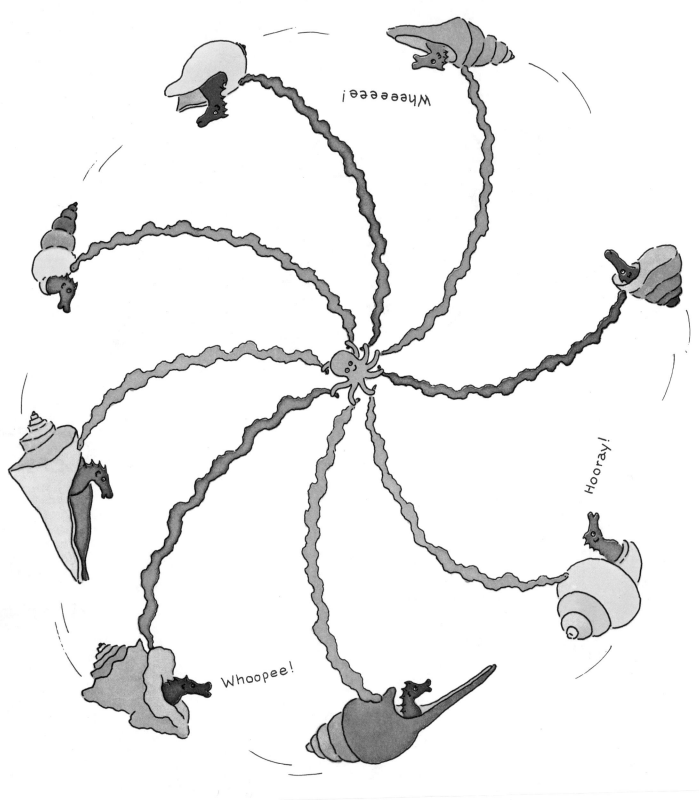

Wheeeee!

Hooray!

Whoopee!

He helped the old.

Whoops!

This will help you swim.

He helped the poor and needy.

Our home is beautiful now.

Thanks to Herman.

He helped the fireman.

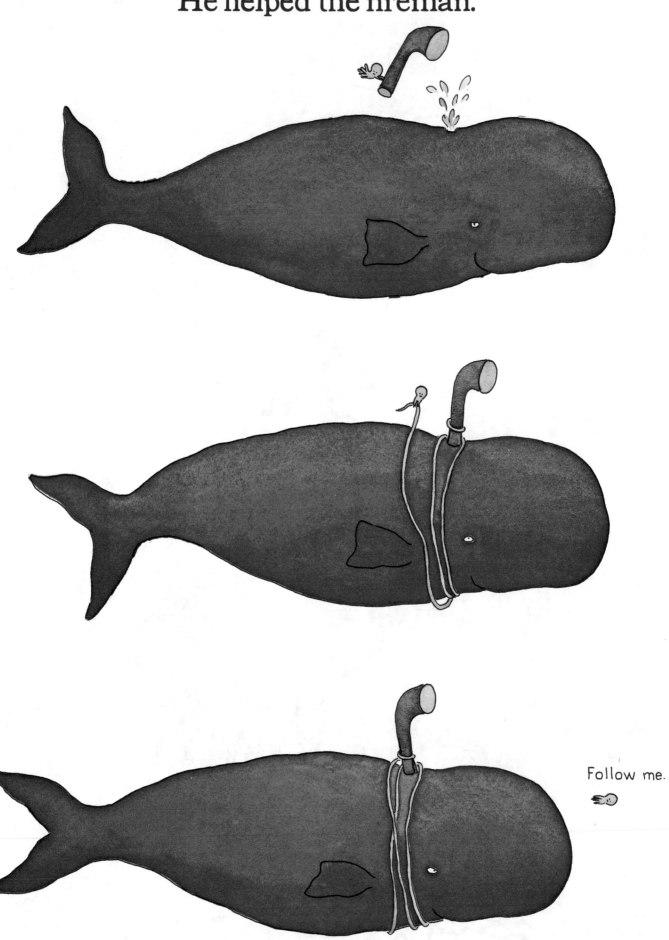

Follow me.

He helped the policeman.

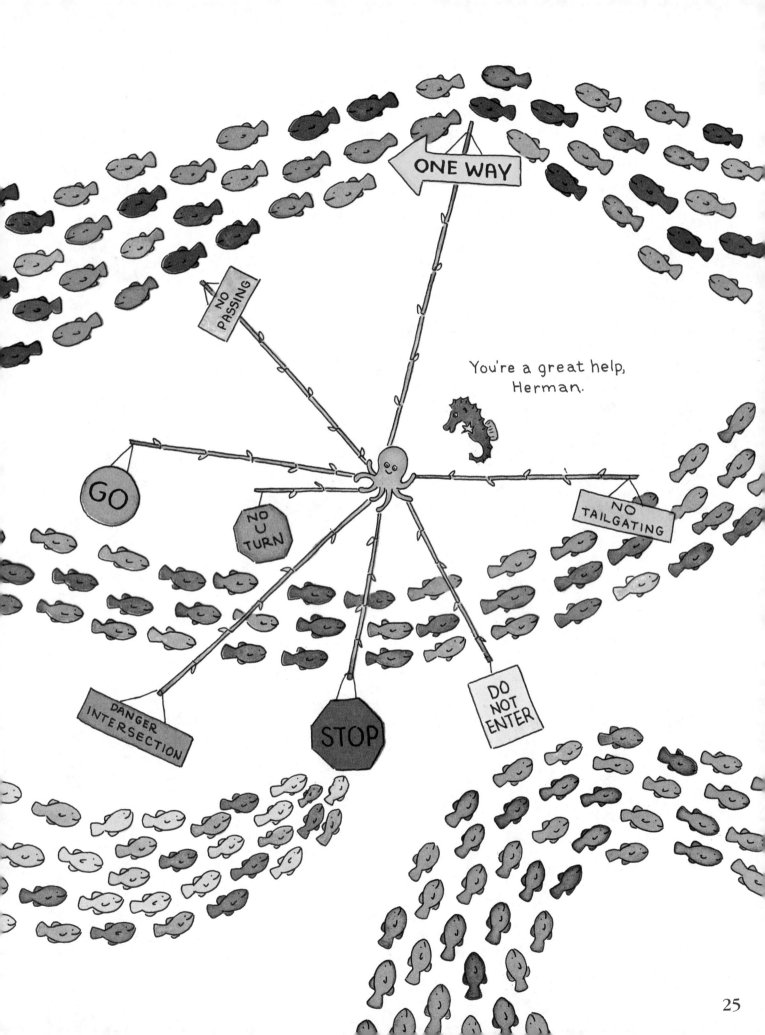

Then the clock struck six and Herman hurried home.

Six o'clock already?

He washed his hands and face.

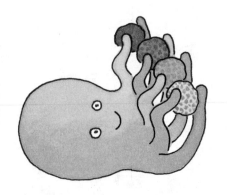

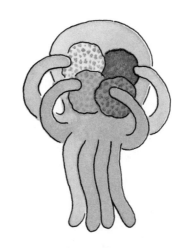

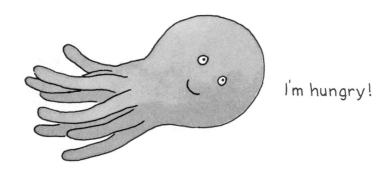

I'm hungry!

And sat down to supper.

"May I help you to some mashed potatoes?"
asked Herman's father.

"No thanks,"
said Herman,
"I'll help myself."

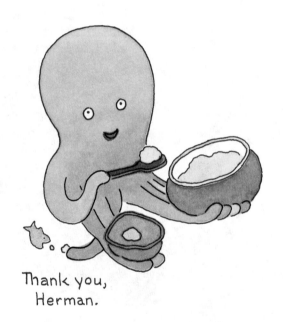

Thank you,
Herman.